Artemis to Actaeon and Other Worlds

Edith Wharton

Contents

I 7
   ARTEMIS TO ACTAEON 7
   LIFE 10
   VESALIUS IN ZANTE 15
   MARGARET OF CORTONA 23
   A TORCHBEARER 29
II 31
   THE MORTAL LEASE 31
   EXPERIENCE 36
   GRIEF 37
   TWO BACKGROUNDS 40
   THE TOMB OF ILARIA GIUNIGI 41
   THE ONE GRIEF 42
   THE EUMENIDES 42
III 44
   ORPHEUS 44
   AN AUTUMN SUNSET 49
   MOONRISE OVER TYRINGHAM 51
   ALL SOULS 54
   ALL SAINTS 57
   THE OLD POLE STAR 59
   A GRAVE 60
   NON DOLET! 62
   A HUNTING-SONG 63
   SURVIVAL 64
   USES 64
   A MEETING 65

ARTEMIS TO ACTAEON AND OTHER WORLDS

BY

Edith Wharton

I

ARTEMIS TO ACTAEON

THOU couldst not look on me and live: so runs
The mortal legend--thou that couldst not live
Nor look on me (so the divine decree)!
That saw'st me in the cloud, the wave, the bough,
The clod commoved with April, and the shapes
Lurking 'twixt lid and eye-ball in the dark.
Mocked I thee not in every guise of life,
Hid in girls' eyes, a naiad in her well,
Wooed through their laughter, and like echo fled,
Luring thee down the primal silences
Where the heart hushes and the flesh is dumb?
Nay, was not I the tide that drew thee out
Relentlessly from the detaining shore,
Forth from the home-lights and the hailing voices,
Forth from the last faint headland's failing line,
Till I enveloped thee from verge to verge
And hid thee in the hollow of my being?
And still, because between us hung the veil,
The myriad-tinted veil of sense, thy feet
Refused their rest, thy hands the gifts of life,
Thy heart its losses, lest some lesser face

Should blur mine image in thine upturned soul
Ere death had stamped it there. This was thy thought.
And mine?

The gods, they say, have all: not so!
This have they--flocks on every hill, the blue
Spirals of incense and the amber drip
Of lucid honey-comb on sylvan shrines,
First-chosen weanlings, doves immaculate,
Twin-cooing in the osier-plaited cage,
And ivy-garlands glaucous with the dew:
Man's wealth, man's servitude, but not himself!
And so they pale, for lack of warmth they wane,
Freeze to the marble of their images,
And, pinnacled on man's subserviency,
Through the thick sacrificial haze discern
Unheeding lives and loves, as some cold peak
Through icy mists may enviously descry
Warm vales unzoned to the all-fruitful sun.
So they along an immortality
Of endless-envistaed homage strain their gaze,
If haply some rash votary, empty-urned,
But light of foot, with all-adventuring hand,
Break rank, fling past the people and the priest,
Up the last step, on to the inmost shrine,
And there, the sacred curtain in his clutch,
Drop dead of seeing--while the others prayed!
Yes, this we wait for, this renews us, this
Incarnates us, pale people of your dreams,
Who are but what you make us, wood or stone,
Or cold chryselephantine hung with gems,
Or else the beating purpose of your life,
Your sword, your clay, the note your pipe pursues,

The face that haunts your pillow, or the light
Scarce visible over leagues of labouring sea!
O thus through use to reign again, to drink
The cup of peradventure to the lees,
For one dear instant disimmortalised
In giving immortality!
So dream the gods upon their listless thrones.
Yet sometimes, when the votary appears,
With death-affronting forehead and glad eyes,
Too young, they rather muse, *too frail thou art,*
And shall we rob some girl of saffron veil
And nuptial garland for so slight a thing?
And so to their incurious loves return.

Not so with thee; for some indeed there are
Who would behold the truth and then return
To pine among the semblances--but I
Divined in thee the questing foot that never
Revisits the cold hearth of yesterday
Or calls achievement home. I from afar
Beheld thee fashioned for one hour's high use,
Nor meant to slake oblivion drop by drop.
Long, long hadst thou inhabited my dreams,
Surprising me as harts surprise a pool,
Stealing to drink at midnight; I divined
Thee rash to reach the heart of life, and lie
Bosom to bosom in occasion's arms.
And said: *Because I love thee thou shalt die!*

For immortality is not to range
Unlimited through vast Olympian days,
Or sit in dull dominion over time;
But this--to drink fate's utmost at a draught,

Nor feel the wine grow stale upon the lip,
To scale the summit of some soaring moment,
Nor know the dulness of the long descent,
To snatch the crown of life and seal it up
Secure forever in the vaults of death!

And this was thine: to lose thyself in me,
Relive in my renewal, and become
The light of other lives, a quenchless torch
Passed on from hand to hand, till men are dust
And the last garland withers from my shrine.

LIFE

NAY, lift me to thy lips, Life, and once more
Pour the wild music through me--

I quivered in the reed-bed with my kind,
Rooted in Lethe-bank, when at the dawn
There came a groping shape of mystery
Moving among us, that with random stroke
Severed, and rapt me from my silent tribe,
Pierced, fashioned, lipped me, sounding for a voice,
Laughing on Lethe-bank--and in my throat
I felt the wing-beat of the fledgeling notes,
The bubble of godlike laughter in my throat.

Such little songs she sang,
Pursing her lips to fit the tiny pipe,

They trickled from me like a slender spring
That strings frail wood-growths on its crystal thread,
Nor dreams of glassing cities, bearing ships.
She sang, and bore me through the April world
Matching the birds, doubling the insect-hum
In the meadows, under the low-moving airs,
And breathings of the scarce-articulate air
When it makes mouths of grasses--but when the sky
Burst into storm, and took great trees for pipes,
She thrust me in her breast, and warm beneath
Her cloudy vesture, on her terrible heart,
I shook, and heard the battle.

But more oft,
Those early days, we moved in charmed woods,
Where once, at dusk, she piped against a faun,
And one warm dawn a tree became a nymph
Listening; and trembled; and Life laughed and passed.
And once we came to a great stream that bore
The stars upon its bosom like a sea,
And ships like stars; so to the sea we came.
And there she raised me to her lips, and sent
One swift pang through me; then refrained her hand,
And whispered: "Hear--" and into my frail flanks,
Into my bursting veins, the whole sea poured
Its spaces and its thunder; and I feared.

We came to cities, and Life piped on me
Low calls to dreaming girls,
In counting-house windows, through the chink of gold,
Flung cries that fired the captive brain of youth,
And made the heavy merchant at his desk
Curse us for a cracked hurdy-gurdy; Life

Mimicked the hurdy-gurdy, and we passed.

We climbed the slopes of solitude, and there
Life met a god, who challenged her and said:
"Thy pipe against my lyre!" But "Wait!" she laughed,
And in my live flank dug a finger-hole,
And wrung new music from it. Ah, the pain!

We climbed and climbed, and left the god behind.
We saw the earth spread vaster than the sea,
With infinite surge of mountains surfed with snow,
And a silence that was louder than the deep;
But on the utmost pinnacle Life again
Hid me, and I heard the terror in her hair.

Safe in new vales, I ached for the old pang,
And clamoured "Play me against a god again!"
"Poor Marsyas-mortal--he shall bleed thee yet,"
She breathed and kissed me, stilling the dim need.
But evermore it woke, and stabbed my flank
With yearnings for new music and new pain.
"Another note against another god!"
I clamoured; and she answered: "Bide my time.
Of every heart-wound I will make a stop,
And drink thy life in music, pang by pang,
But first thou must yield the notes I stored in thee
At dawn beside the river. Take my lips."

She kissed me like a lover, but I wept,
Remembering that high song against the god,
And the old songs slept in me, and I was dumb.

We came to cavernous foul places, blind
With harpy-wings, and sulphurous with the glare
Of sinful furnaces--where hunger toiled,
And pleasure gathered in a starveling prey,
And death fed delicately on young bones.

"Now sing!" cried Life, and set her lips to me.
"Here are gods also. Wilt thou pipe for Dis?"
My cry was drowned beneath the furnace roar,
Choked by the sulphur-fumes; and beast-lipped gods
Laughed down on me, and mouthed the flutes of hell.

"Now sing!" said Life, reissuing to the stars;
And wrung a new note from my wounded side.

So came we to clear spaces, and the sea.
And now I felt its volume in my heart,
And my heart waxed with it, and Life played on me
The song of the Infinite. "Now the stars," she said.

Then from the utmost pinnacle again
She poured me on the wild sidereal stream,
And I grew with her great breathings, till we swept
The interstellar spaces like new worlds
Loosed from the fiery ruin of a star.

Cold, cold we rested on black peaks again,
Under black skies, under a groping wind;
And Life, grown old, hugged me to a numb breast,
Pressing numb lips against me. Suddenly
A blade of silver severed the black peaks
From the black sky, and earth was born again,
Breathing and various, under a god's feet.

A god! A god! I felt the heart of Life
Leap under me, and my cold flanks shook again.
He bore no lyre, he rang no challenge out,
But Life warmed to him, warming me with her,
And as he neared I felt beneath her hands
The stab of a new wound that sucked my soul
Forth in a new song from my throbbing throat.

"His name--his name?" I whispered, but she shed
The music faster, and I grew with it,
Became a part of it, while Life and I
Clung lip to lip, and I from her wrung song
As she from me, one song, one ecstasy,
In indistinguishable union blent,
Till she became the flute and I the player.
And lo! the song I played on her was more
Than any she had drawn from me; it held
The stars, the peaks, the cities, and the sea,
The faun's catch, the nymph's tremor, and the heart
Of dreaming girls, of toilers at the desk,
Apollo's challenge on the sunrise slope,
And the hiss of the night-gods mouthing flutes of hell--
All, to the dawn-wind's whisper in the reeds,
When Life first came, a shape of mystery,
Moving among us, and with random stroke
Severed, and rapt me from my silent tribe.
All this I wrung from her in that deep hour,
While Love stood murmuring: "Play the god, poor grass!"

Now, by that hour, I am a mate to thee
Forever, Life, however spent and clogged,
And tossed back useless to my native mud!
Yea, groping for new reeds to fashion thee

New instruments of anguish and delight,
Thy hand shall leap to me, thy broken reed,
Thine ear remember me, thy bosom thrill
With the old subjection, then when Love and I
Held thee, and fashioned thee, and made thee dance
Like a slave-girl to her pipers--yea, thou yet
Shalt hear my call, and dropping all thy toys
Thou'lt lift me to thy lips, Life, and once more
Pour the wild music through me--

VESALIUS IN ZANTE (See note at end)
(1564)

SET wide the window. Let me drink the day.
I loved light ever, light in eye and brain--
No tapers mirrored in long palace floors,
Nor dedicated depths of silent aisles,
But just the common dusty wind-blown day
That roofs earth's millions.

O, too long I walked
In that thrice-sifted air that princes breathe,
Nor felt the heaven-wide jostling of the winds
And all the ancient outlawry of earth!
Now let me breathe and see.

This pilgrimage
They call a penance--let them call it that!
I set my face to the East to shrive my soul

Of mortal sin? So be it. If my blade
Once questioned living flesh, if once I tore
The pages of the Book in opening it,
See what the torn page yielded ere the light
Had paled its buried characters--and judge!

The girl they brought me, pinioned hand and foot
In catalepsy--say I should have known
That trance had not yet darkened into death,
And held my scalpel. Well, suppose I **knew?**
Sum up the facts--her life against her death.
Her life? The scum upon the pools of pleasure
Breeds such by thousands. And her death? Perchance
The obolus to appease the ferrying Shade,
And waft her into immortality.
Think what she purchased with that one heart-flutter
That whispered its deep secret to my blade!
For, just because her bosom fluttered still,
It told me more than many rifled graves;
Because I spoke too soon, she answered me,
Her vain life ripened to this bud of death
As the whole plant is forced into one flower,
All her blank past a scroll on which God wrote
His word of healing--so that the poor flesh,
Which spread death living, died to purchase life!

Ah, no! The sin I sinned was mine, not theirs.
Not **that** they sent me forth to wash away--
None of their tariffed frailties, but a deed
So far beyond their grasp of good or ill
That, set to weigh it in the Church's balance,
Scarce would they know which scale to cast it in.
But I, I know. I sinned against my will,

Myself, my soul--the God within the breast:
Can any penance wash such sacrilege?

When I was young in Venice, years ago,
I walked the hospice with a Spanish monk,
A solitary cloistered in high thoughts,
The great Loyola, whom I reckoned then
A mere refurbisher of faded creeds,
Expert to edge anew the arms of faith,
As who should say, a Galenist, resolved
To hold the walls of dogma against fact,
Experience, insight, his own self, if need be!
Ah, how I pitied him, mine own eyes set
Straight in the level beams of Truth, who groped
In error's old deserted catacombs
And lit his tapers upon empty graves!
Ay, but he held his own, the monk--more man
Than any laurelled cripple of the wars,
Charles's spent shafts; for what he willed he willed,
As those do that forerun the wheels of fate,
Not take their dust--that force the virgin hours,
Hew life into the likeness of themselves
And wrest the stars from their concurrences.
So firm his mould; but mine the ductile soul
That wears the livery of circumstance
And hangs obsequious on its suzerain's eye.
For who rules now? The twilight-flitting monk,
Or I, that took the morning like an Alp?
He held his own, I let mine slip from me,
The birthright that no sovereign can restore;
And so ironic Time beholds us now
Master and slave--he lord of half the earth,
I ousted from my narrow heritage.

For there's the sting! My kingdom knows me not.
Reach me that folio--my usurper's title!
Fallopius reigning, *vice*--nay, not so:
Successor, not usurper. I am dead.
My throne stood empty; he was heir to it.
Ay, but who hewed his kingdom from the waste,
Cleared, inch by inch, the acres for his sowing,
Won back for man that ancient fief o' the Church,
His body? Who flung Galen from his seat,
And founded the great dynasty of truth
In error's central kingdom?

Ask men that,
And see their answer: just a wondering stare
To learn things were not always as they are--
The very fight forgotten with the fighter;
Already grows the moss upon my grave!
Ay, and so meet--hold fast to that, Vesalius.
They only, who re-conquer day by day
The inch of ground they camped on over-night,
Have right of foothold on this crowded earth.
I left mine own; he seized it; with it went
My name, my fame, my very self, it seems,
Till I am but the symbol of a man,
The sign-board creaking o'er an empty inn.
He names me--true! ***Oh, give the door its due***
I entered by. Only, I pray you, note,
Had door been none, a shoulder-thrust of mine
Had breached the crazy wall"--he seems to say.
So meet--and yet a word of thanks, of praise,
Of recognition that the clue was found,
Seized, followed, clung to, by some hand now dust--
Had this obscured his quartering of my shield?

How the one weakness stirs again! I thought
I had done with that old thirst for gratitude
That lured me to the desert years ago.
I did my work--and was not that enough?
No; but because the idlers sneered and shrugged,
The envious whispered, the traducers lied,
And friendship doubted where it should have cheered
I flung aside the unfinished task, sought praise
Outside my soul's esteem, and learned too late
That victory, like God's kingdom, is within.
(Nay, let the folio rest upon my knee.
I do not feel its weight.) Ingratitude?
The hurrying traveller does not ask the name
Of him who points him on his way; and this
Fallopius sits in the mid-heart of me,
Because he keeps his eye upon the goal,
Cuts a straight furrow to the end in view,
Cares not who oped the fountain by the way,
But drinks to draw fresh courage for his journey.
That was the lesson that Ignatius taught--
The one I might have learned from him, but would not--
That we are but stray atoms on the wind,
A dancing transiency of summer eves,
Till we become one with our purpose, merged
In that vast effort of the race which makes
Mortality immortal.

   "He that loseth
His life shall find it": so the Scripture runs.
But I so hugged the fleeting self in me,
So loved the lovely perishable hours,
So kissed myself to death upon their lips,
That on one pyre we perished in the end--

A grimmer bonfire than the Church e'er lit!
Yet all was well--or seemed so--till I heard
That younger voice, an echo of my own,
And, like a wanderer turning to his home,
Who finds another on the hearth, and learns,
Half-dazed, that other is his actual self
In name and claim, as the whole parish swears,
So strangely, suddenly, stood dispossessed
Of that same self I had sold all to keep,
A baffled ghost that none would see or hear!
"Vesalius? Who's Vesalius? This Fallopius
It is who dragged the Galen-idol down,
Who rent the veil of flesh and forced a way
Into the secret fortalice of life"--
Yet it was I that bore the brunt of it!

Well, better so! Better awake and live
My last brief moment as the man I was,
Than lapse from life's long lethargy to death
Without one conscious interval. At least
I repossess my past, am once again
No courtier med'cining the whims of kings
In muffled palace-chambers, but the free
Friendless Vesalius, with his back to the wall
And all the world against him. O, for that
Best gift of all, Fallopius, take my thanks--
That, and much more. At first, when Padua wrote:
"Master, Fallopius dead, resume again
The chair even he could not completely fill,
And see what usury age shall take of youth
In honours forfeited"--why, just at first,
I was quite simply credulously glad
To think the old life stood ajar for me,

Like a fond woman's unforgetting heart.
But now that death waylays me--now I know
This isle is the circumference of my days,
And I shall die here in a little while--
So also best, Fallopius!

For I see
The gods may give anew, but not restore;
And though I think that, in my chair again,
I might have argued my supplanters wrong
In this or that--this Cesalpinus, say,
With all his hot-foot blundering in the dark,
Fabricius, with his over-cautious clutch
On Galen (systole and diastole
Of Truth's mysterious heart!)--yet, other ways,
It may be that this dying serves the cause.
For Truth stays not to build her monument
For this or that co-operating hand,
But props it with her servants' failures--nay,
Cements its courses with their blood and brains,
A living substance that shall clinch her walls
Against the assaults of time. Already, see,
Her scaffold rises on my hidden toil,
I but the accepted premiss whence must spring
The airy structure of her argument;
Nor could the bricks it rests on serve to build
The crowning finials. I abide her law:
A different substance for a different end--
Content to know I hold the building up;
Though men, agape at dome and pinnacles,
Guess not, the whole must crumble like a dream
But for that buried labour underneath.
Yet, Padua, I had still my word to say!

Let others say it!--Ah, but will they guess
Just the one word--? Nay, Truth is many-tongued.
What one man failed to speak, another finds
Another word for. May not all converge
In some vast utterance, of which you and I,
Fallopius, were but halting syllables?
So knowledge come, no matter how it comes!
No matter whence the light falls, so it fall!
Truth's way, not mine--that I, whose service failed
In action, yet may make amends in praise.
Fabricius, Cesalpinus, say your word,
Not yours, or mine, but Truth's, as you receive it!
You miss a point I saw? See others, then!
Misread my meaning? Yet expound your own!
Obscure one space I cleared? The sky is wide,
And you may yet uncover other stars.
For thus I read the meaning of this end:
There are two ways of spreading light: to be
The candle or the mirror that reflects it.
I let my wick burn out--there yet remains
To spread an answering surface to the flame
That others kindle.

Turn me in my bed.
The window darkens as the hours swing round;
But yonder, look, the other casement glows!
Let me face westward as my sun goes down.

MARGARET OF CORTONA

FRA PAOLO, since they say the end is near,
And you of all men have the gentlest eyes,
Most like our father Francis; since you know
How I have toiled and prayed and scourged and striven,
Mothered the orphan, waked beside the sick,
Gone empty that mine enemy might eat,
Given bread for stones in famine years, and channelled
With vigilant knees the pavement of this cell,
Till I constrained the Christ upon the wall
To bend His thorn-crowned Head in mute forgiveness . . .
Three times He bowed it . . . (but the whole stands writ,
Sealed with the Bishop's signet, as you know),
Once for each person of the Blessed Three--
A miracle that the whole town attests,
The very babes thrust forward for my blessing,
And either parish plotting for my bones--
Since this you know: sit near and bear with me.

I have lain here, these many empty days
I thought to pack with Credos and Hail Marys
So close that not a fear should force the door--
But still, between the blessed syllables
That taper up like blazing angel heads,
Praise over praise, to the Unutterable,
Strange questions clutch me, thrusting fiery arms,
As though, athwart the close-meshed litanies,
My dead should pluck at me from hell, with eyes
Alive in their obliterated faces! . . .
I have tried the saints' names and our blessed Mother's

Fra Paolo, I have tried them o'er and o'er,
And like a blade bent backward at first thrust
They yield and fail me--and the questions stay.
And so I thought, into some human heart,
Pure, and yet foot-worn with the tread of sin,
If only I might creep for sanctuary,
It might be that those eyes would let me rest. . .

Fra Paolo, listen. How should I forget
The day I saw him first? (You know the one.)
I had been laughing in the market-place
With others like me, I the youngest there,
Jostling about a pack of mountebanks
Like flies on carrion (I the youngest there!),
Till darkness fell; and while the other girls
Turned this way, that way, as perdition beckoned,
I, wondering what the night would bring, half hoping:
If not, this once, a child's sleep in my garret,
At least enough to buy that two-pronged coral
The others covet 'gainst the evil eye,
Since, after all, one sees that I'm the youngest--
So, muttering my litany to hell
(The only prayer I knew that was not Latin),
Felt on my arm a touch as kind as yours,
And heard a voice as kind as yours say "Come."
I turned and went; and from that day I never
Looked on the face of any other man.
So much is known; so much effaced; the sin
Cast like a plague-struck body to the sea,
Deep, deep into the unfathomable pardon--
(The Head bowed thrice, as the whole town attests).
What more, then? To what purpose? Bear with me!--

It seems that he, a stranger in the place,
First noted me that afternoon and wondered:
How grew so white a bud in such black slime,
And why not mine the hand to pluck it out?
Why, so Christ deals with souls, you cry--what then?
Not so! Not so! When Christ, the heavenly gardener,
Plucks flowers for Paradise (do I not know?),
He snaps the stem above the root, and presses
The ransomed soul between two convent walls,
A lifeless blossom in the Book of Life.
But when my lover gathered me, he lifted
Stem, root and all--ay, and the clinging mud--
And set me on his sill to spread and bloom
After the common way, take sun and rain,
And make a patch of brightness for the street,
Though raised above rough fingers--so you make
A weed a flower, and others, passing, think:
"Next ditch I cross, I'll lift a root from it,
And dress my window" . . . and the blessing spreads.
Well, so I grew, with every root and tendril
Grappling the secret anchorage of his love,
And so we loved each other till he died. . . .

Ah, that black night he left me, that dead dawn
I found him lying in the woods, alive
To gasp my name out and his life-blood with it,
As though the murderer's knife had probed for me
In his hacked breast and found me in each wound. . .
Well, it was there Christ came to me, you know,
And led me home--just as that other led me.
(Just as that other? Father, bear with me!)
My lover's death, they tell me, saved my soul,
And I have lived to be a light to men.

And gather sinners to the knees of grace.
All this, you say, the Bishop's signet covers.
But stay! Suppose my lover had not died?
(At last my question! Father, help me face it.)
I say: Suppose my lover had not died--
Think you I ever would have left him living,
Even to be Christ's blessed Margaret?
--We lived in sin? Why, to the sin I died to
That other was as Paradise, when God
Walks there at eventide, the air pure gold,
And angels treading all the grass to flowers!
He was my Christ--he led me out of hell--
He died to save me (so your casuists say!)--
Could Christ do more? Your Christ out-pity mine?
Why, **yours** but let the sinner bathe His feet;
Mine raised her to the level of his heart. . .
And then Christ's way is saving, as man's way
Is squandering--and the devil take the shards!
But this man kept for sacramental use
The cup that once had slaked a passing thirst;
This man declared: "The same clay serves to model
A devil or a saint; the scribe may stain
The same fair parchment with obscenities,
Or gild with benedictions; nay," he cried,
"Because a satyr feasted in this wood,
And fouled the grasses with carousing foot,
Shall not a hermit build his chapel here
And cleanse the echoes with his litanies?
The sodden grasses spring again--why not
The trampled soul? Is man less merciful
Than nature, good more fugitive than grass?"
And so--if, after all, he had not died,
And suddenly that door should know his hand,

And with that voice as kind as yours he said:
"Come, Margaret, forth into the sun again,
Back to the life we fashioned with our hands
Out of old sins and follies, fragments scorned
Of more ambitious builders, yet by Love,
The patient architect, so shaped and fitted
That not a crevice let the winter in--"
Think you my bones would not arise and walk,
This bruised body (as once the bruised soul)
Turn from the wonders of the seventh heaven
As from the antics of the market-place?
If this could be (as I so oft have dreamed),
I, who have known both loves, divine and human,
Think you I would not leave this Christ for that?

--I rave, you say? You start from me, Fra Paolo?
Go, then; your going leaves me not alone.
I marvel, rather, that I feared the question,
Since, now I name it, it draws near to me
With such dear reassurance in its eyes,
And takes your place beside me. . .

Nay, I tell you,
Fra Paolo, I have cried on all the saints--
If this be devil's prompting, let them drown it
In Alleluias! Yet not one replies.
And, for the Christ there--is He silent too?
Your Christ? Poor father; you that have but one,
And that one silent--how I pity you!
He will not answer? Will not help you cast
The devil out? But hangs there on the wall,
Blind wood and bone--?

How if *I* call on Him--
I, whom He talks with, as the town attests?
If ever prayer hath ravished me so high
That its wings failed and dropped me in Thy breast,
Christ, I adjure Thee! By that naked hour
Of innermost commixture, when my soul
Contained Thee as the paten holds the host,
Judge Thou alone between this priest and me;
Nay, rather, Lord, between my past and present,
Thy Margaret and that other's--whose she is
By right of salvage--and whose call should follow!
Thine? Silent still.--Or his, who stooped to her,
And drew her to Thee by the bands of love?
Not Thine? Then his?

Ah, Christ--the thorn-crowned Head
Bends . . . bends again . . . down on your knees,

Fra Paolo!
If his, then Thine!

Kneel, priest, for this is heaven. . .

A TORCHBEARER

GREAT cities rise and have their fall; the brass
That held their glories moulders in its turn.
Hard granite rots like an uprooted weed,
And ever on the palimpsest of earth
Impatient Time rubs out the word he writ.
But one thing makes the years its pedestal,
Springs from the ashes of its pyre, and claps
A skyward wing above its epitaph--
The will of man willing immortal things.

The ages are but baubles hung upon
The thread of some strong lives--and one slight wrist
May lift a century above the dust;
For Time,
The Sisyphean load of little lives,
Becomes the globe and sceptre of the great.
But who are these that, linking hand in hand,
Transmit across the twilight waste of years
The flying brightness of a kindled hour?
Not always, nor alone, the lives that search
How they may snatch a glory out of heaven
Or add a height to Babel; oftener they
That in the still fulfilment of each day's
Pacific order hold great deeds in leash,
That in the sober sheath of tranquil tasks
Hide the attempered blade of high emprise,
And leap like lightning to the clap of fate.

So greatly gave he, nurturing 'gainst the call
Of one rare moment all the daily store
Of joy distilled from the acquitted task,
And that deliberate rashness which bespeaks
The pondered action passed into the blood;
So swift to harden purpose into deed
That, with the wind of ruin in his hair,
Soul sprang full-statured from the broken flesh,
And at one stroke he lived the whole of life,
Poured all in one libation to the truth,
A brimming flood whose drops shall overflow
On deserts of the soul long beaten down
By the brute hoof of habit, till they spring
In manifold upheaval to the sun.

Call here no high artificer to raise
His wordy monument--such lives as these
Make death a dull misnomer and its pomp
An empty vesture. Let resounding lives
Re-echo splendidly through high-piled vaults
And make the grave their spokesman--such as he
Are as the hidden streams that, underground,
Sweeten the pastures for the grazing kine,
Or as spring airs that bring through prison bars
The scent of freedom; or a light that burns
Immutably across the shaken seas,
Forevermore by nameless hands renewed,
Where else were darkness and a glutted shore.

II

THE MORTAL LEASE

I

BECAUSE the currents of our love are poured
Through the slow welter of the primal flood
From some blind source of monster-haunted mud,
And flung together by random forces stored
Ere the vast void with rushing worlds was scored--
Because we know ourselves but the dim scud
Tossed from their heedless keels, the sea-blown bud
That wastes and scatters ere the wave has roared--

Because we have this knowledge in our veins,
Shall we deny the journey's gathered lore--
The great refusals and the long disdains,
The stubborn questing for a phantom shore,
The sleepless hopes and memorable pains,
And all mortality's immortal gains?

II

Because our kiss is as the moon to draw
The mounting waters of that red-lit sea
That circles brain with sense, and bids us be
The playthings of an elemental law,
Shall we forego the deeper touch of awe
On love's extremest pinnacle, where we,
Winging the vistas of infinity,
Gigantic on the mist our shadows saw?

Shall kinship with the dim first-moving clod
Not draw the folded pinion from the soul,
And shall we not, by spirals vision-trod,
Reach upward to some still-retreating goal,
As earth, escaping from the night's control,
Drinks at the founts of morning like a god?

III

All, all is sweet in that commingled draught
Mysterious, that life pours for lovers' thirst,
And I would meet your passion as the first
Wild woodland woman met her captor's craft,
Or as the Greek whose fearless beauty laughed
And doffed her raiment by the Attic flood;
But in the streams of my belated blood
Flow all the warring potions love has quaffed.

How can I be to you the nymph who danced
Smooth by Ilissus as the plane-tree's bole,
Or how the Nereid whose drenched lashes glanced

Like sea-flowers through the summer sea's long roll--
I that have also been the nun entranced
Who night-long held her Bridegroom in her soul?

IV

"Sad Immortality is dead," you say,
"And all her grey brood banished from the soul;
Life, like the earth, is now a rounded whole,
The orb of man's dominion. Live to-day."
And every sense in me leapt to obey,
Seeing the routed phantoms backward roll;
But from their waning throng a whisper stole,
And touched the morning splendour with decay.

"Sad Immortality is dead; and we
The funeral train that bear her to her grave.
Yet hath she left a two-faced progeny
In hearts of men, and some will always see
The skull beneath the wreath, yet always crave
In every kiss the folded kiss to be."

V

Yet for one rounded moment I will be
No more to you than what my lips may give,
And in the circle of your kisses live
As in some island of a storm-blown sea,
Where the cold surges of infinity
Upon the outward reefs unheeded grieve,
And the loud murmur of our blood shall weave

Primeval silences round you and me.

If in that moment we are all we are
We live enough. Let this for all requite.
Do I not know, some winged things from far
Are borne along illimitable night
To dance their lives out in a single flight
Between the moonrise and the setting star?

VI

The Moment came, with sacramental cup
Lifted--and all the vault of life grew bright
With tides of incommensurable light--
But tremblingly I turned and covered up
My face before the wonder. Down the slope
I heard her feet in irretrievable flight,
And when I looked again, my stricken sight
Saw night and rain in a dead world agrope.

Now walks her ghost beside me, whispering
With lips derisive: "Thou that wouldst forego--
What god assured thee that the cup I bring
Globes not in every drop the cosmic show,
All that the insatiate heart of man can wring
From life's long vintage?--Now thou shalt not know."

VII

Shall I not know? I, that could always catch
The sunrise in one beam along the wall,

The nests of June in April's mating call,
And ruinous autumn in the wind's first snatch
At summer's green impenetrable thatch--
That always knew far off the secret fall
Of a god's feet across the city's brawl,
The touch of silent fingers on my latch?

Not thou, vain Moment! Something more than thou
Shall write the score of what mine eyes have wept,
The touch of kisses that have missed my brow,
The murmur of wings that brushed me while I slept,
And some mute angel in the breast even now
Measures my loss by all that I have kept.

VIII

Strive we no more. Some hearts are like the bright
Tree-chequered spaces, flecked with sun and shade,
Where gathered in old days the youth and maid
To woo, and weave their dances: with the night
They cease their flutings, and the next day's light
Finds the smooth green unconscious of their tread,
And ready its velvet pliancies to spread
Under fresh feet, till these in turn take flight.

But other hearts a long long road doth span,
From some far region of old works and wars,
And the weary armies of the thoughts of man
Have trampled it, and furrowed it with scars,
And sometimes, husht, a sacred caravan
Moves over it alone, beneath the stars.

EXPERIENCE

I

LIKE Crusoe with the bootless gold we stand
Upon the desert verge of death, and say:
"What shall avail the woes of yesterday
To buy to-morrow's wisdom, in the land
Whose currency is strange unto our hand?
In life's small market they had served to pay
Some late-found rapture, could we but delay
Till Time hath matched our means to our demand."

But otherwise Fate wills it, for, behold,
Our gathered strength of individual pain,
When Time's long alchemy hath made it gold,
Dies with us--hoarded all these years in vain,
Since those that might be heir to it the mould
Renew, and coin themselves new griefs again.

II

O Death, we come full-handed to thy gate,
Rich with strange burden of the mingled years,
Gains and renunciations, mirth and tears,
And love's oblivion, and remembering hate.
Nor know we what compulsion laid such freight
Upon our souls--and shall our hopes and fears
Buy nothing of thee, Death? Behold our wares,
And sell us the one joy for which we wait.

Had we lived longer, life had such for sale,
With the last coin of sorrow purchased cheap,
But now we stand before thy shadowy pale,
And all our longings lie within thy keep--
Death, can it be the years shall naught avail?

"Not so," Death answered, "they shall purchase sleep."

GRIEF

I

ON immemorial altitudes august
Grief holds her high dominion. Bold the feet
That climb unblenching to that stern retreat
Whence, looking down, man knows himself but dust.
There lie the mightiest passions, earthward thrust
Beneath her regnant footstool, and there meet
Pale ghosts of buried longings that were sweet,
With many an abdicated "shall" and "must."

For there she rules omnipotent, whose will
Compels a mute acceptance of her chart;
Who holds the world, and lo! it cannot fill
Her mighty hand; who will be served apart
With uncommunicable rites, and still
Surrender of the undivided heart.

II

She holds the world within her mighty hand,
And lo! it is a toy for babes to toss,
And all its shining imagery but dross,
To those that in her awful presence stand;
As sun-confronting eagles o'er the land
That lies below, they send their gaze across
The common intervals of gain and loss,
And hope's infinitude without a strand.

But he who, on that lonely eminence,
Watches too long the whirling of the spheres
Through dim eternities, descending thence
The voices of his kind no longer hears,
And, blinded by the spectacle immense,
Journeys alone through all the after years.

CHARTRES

I

IMMENSE, august, like some Titanic bloom,
The mighty choir unfolds its lithic core,
Petalled with panes of azure, gules and or,
Splendidly lambent in the Gothic gloom,
And stamened with keen flamelets that illume
The pale high-altar. On the prayer-worn floor,
By worshippers innumerous thronged of yore,

A few brown crones, familiars of the tomb,
The stranded driftwood of Faith's ebbing sea--
For these alone the finials fret the skies,
The topmost bosses shake their blossoms free,
While from the triple portals, with grave eyes,
Tranquil, and fixed upon eternity,
The cloud of witnesses still testifies.

II

The crimson panes like blood-drops stigmatise
The western floor. The aisles are mute and cold.
A rigid fetich in her robe of gold,
The Virgin of the Pillar, with blank eyes,
Enthroned beneath her votive canopies,
Gathers a meagre remnant to her fold.
The rest is solitude; the church, grown old,
Stands stark and grey beneath the burning skies.
Well-nigh again its mighty framework grows
To be a part of nature's self, withdrawn
From hot humanity's impatient woes;
The floor is ridged like some rude mountain lawn,
And in the east one giant window shows
The roseate coldness of an Alp at dawn.

TWO BACKGROUNDS

I

LA VIERGE AU DONATEUR

HERE by the ample river's argent sweep,
Bosomed in tilth and vintage to her walls,
A tower-crowned Cybele in armoured sleep
The city lies, fat plenty in her halls,
With calm parochial spires that hold in fee
The friendly gables clustered at their base,
And, equipoised o'er tower and market-place,
The Gothic minister's winged immensity;
And in that narrow burgh, with equal mood,
Two placid hearts, to all life's good resigned,
Might, from the altar to the lych-gate, find
Long years of peace and dreamless plenitude.

II

MONA LISA

Yon strange blue city crowns a scarped steep
No mortal foot hath bloodlessly essayed:
Dreams and illusions beacon from its keep.
But at the gate an Angel bares his blade;
And tales are told of those who thought to gain

At dawn its ramparts; but when evening fell
Far off they saw each fading pinnacle
Lit with wild lightnings from the heaven of pain;
Yet there two souls, whom life's perversities
Had mocked with want in plenty, tears in mirth,
Might meet in dreams, ungarmented of earth,
And drain Joy's awful chalice to the lees.

THE TOMB OF ILARIA GIUNIGI

ILARIA, thou that wert so fair and dear
That death would fain disown thee, grief made wise
With prophecy thy husband's widowed eyes,
And bade him call the master's art to rear
Thy perfect image on the sculptured bier,
With dreaming lids, hands laid in peaceful guise
Beneath the breast that seems to fall and rise,
And lips that at love's call should answer "Here!"

First-born of the Renascence, when thy soul
Cast the sweet robing of the flesh aside,
Into these lovelier marble limbs it stole,
Regenerate in art's sunrise clear and wide,
As saints who, having kept faith's raiment whole,
Change it above for garments glorified.

THE ONE GRIEF

ONE grief there is, the helpmeet of my heart,
That shall not from me till my days be sped,
That walks beside me in sunshine and in shade,
And hath in all my fortunes equal part.
At first I feared it, and would often start
Aghast to find it bending o'er my bed,
Till usage slowly dulled the edge of dread,
And one cold night I cried: ***How warm thou art!***

Since then we two have travelled hand in hand,
And, lo, my grief has been interpreter
For me in many a fierce and alien land
Whose speech young Joy had failed to understand,
Plucking me tribute of red gold and myrrh
From desolate whirlings of the desert sand.

THE EUMENIDES

THINK you we slept within the Delphic bower,
What time our victim sought Apollo's grace?
Nay, drawn into ourselves, in that deep place
Where good and evil meet, we bode our hour.
For not inexorable is our power.
And we are hunted of the prey we chase,

Soonest gain ground on them that flee apace,
And draw temerity from hearts that cower.

Shuddering we gather in the house of ruth,
And on the fearful turn a face of fear,
But they to whom the ways of doom are clear
Not vainly named us the Eumenides.
Our feet are faithful in the paths of truth,
And in the constant heart we house at peace.

III

ORPHEUS

Love will make men dare to die for their beloved. . . Of this
Alcestis is a monument . . . for she was willing to lay down her
life for her husband . . . and so noble did this appear to the gods
that they granted her the privilege of returning to earth . . . but
Orpheus, the son of OEagrus, they sent empty away. . .

--PLATO: *The Symposium.*

    ORPHEUS the Harper, coming to the gate
    Where thc implacable dim warder sate,
    Besought for parley with a shade within,
    Dearer to him than life itself had been,
    Sweeter than sunlight on Illyrian sea,
    Or bloom of myrtle, or murmur of laden bee,
    Whom lately from his unconsenting breast
    The Fates, at some capricious blind behest,
    Intolerably had reft--Eurydice,
    Dear to the sunlight as Illyrian sea,
    Sweet as the murmur of bees, or myrtle bloom--

And uncompanioned led her to the tomb.

There, solitary by the Stygian tide,
Strayed her dear feet, the shadow of his own,
Since, 'mid the desolate millions who have died,
Each phantom walks its crowded path alone;
And there her head, that slept upon his breast,
No more had such sweet harbour for its rest,
Nor her swift ear from those disvoiced throats
Could catch one echo of his living notes,
And, dreaming nightly of her pallid doom,
No solace had he of his own young bloom,
But yearned to pour his blood into her veins
And buy her back with unimagined pains.

To whom the Shepherd of the Shadows said:
"Yea, many thus would bargain for their dead;
But when they hear my fatal gateway clang
Life quivers in them with a last sweet pang.
They see the smoke of home above the trees,
The cordage whistles on the harbour breeze;
The beaten path that wanders to the shore
Grows dear because they shall not tread it more,
The dog that drowsing on their threshold lies
Looks at them with their childhood in his eyes,
And in the sunset's melancholy fall
They read a sunrise that shall give them all."

"Not thus am I," the Harper smiled his scorn.
"I see no path but those her feet have worn;
My roof-tree is the shadow of her hair,
And the light breaking through her long despair
The only sunrise that mine eyelids crave;

For doubly dead without me in the grave
Is she who, if my feet had gone before,
Had found life dark as death's abhorred shore."

The gate clanged on him, and he went his way
Amid the alien millions, mute and grey,
Swept like a cold mist down an unlit strand,
Where nameless wreckage gluts the stealthy sand,
Drift of the cockle-shells of hope and faith
Wherein they foundered on the rock of death.

So came he to the image that he sought
(Less living than her semblance in his thought),
Who, at the summons of his thrilling notes,
Drew back to life as a drowned creature floats
Back to the surface; yet no less is dead.
And cold fear smote him till she spoke and said:
"Art thou then come to lay thy lips on mine,
And pour thy life's libation out like wine?
Shall I, through thee, revisit earth again,
Traverse the shining sea, the fruitful plain,
Behold the house we dwelt in, lay my head
Upon the happy pillows of our bed,
And feel in dreams the pressure of thine arms
Kindle these pulses that no memory warms?
Nay: give me for a space upon thy breast
Death's shadowy substitute for rapture--rest;
Then join again the joyous living throng,
And give me life, but give it in thy song;
For only they that die themselves may give
Life to the dead: and I would have thee live."

Fear seized him closer than her arms; but he
Answered: "Not so--for thou shalt come with me!
I sought thee not that we should part again,
But that fresh joy should bud from the old pain;
And the gods, if grudgingly their gifts they make,
Yield all to them that without asking take."

"The gods," she said, "(so runs life's ancient lore)
Yield all man takes, but always claim their score.
The iron wings of the Eumenides
When heard far off seem but a summer breeze;
But me thou'lt have alive on earth again
Only by paying here my meed of pain.
Then lay on my cold lips the tender ghost
Of the dear kiss that used to warm them most,
Take from my frozen hands thy hands of fire,
And of my heart-strings make thee a new lyre,
That in thy music men may find my voice,
And something of me still on earth rejoice."

Shuddering he heard her, but with close-flung arm
Swept her resisting through the ghostly swarm.
"Swift, hide thee 'neath my cloak, that we may glide
Past the dim warder as the gate swings wide."
He whirled her with him, lighter than a leaf
Unwittingly whirled onward by a brief
Autumnal eddy; but when the fatal door
Suddenly yielded him to life once more,
And issuing to the all-consoling skies
He turned to seek the sunlight in her eyes,
He clutched at emptiness--she was not there;
And the dim warder answered to his prayer:
"Only once have I seen the wonder wrought.

But when Alcestis thus her master sought,
Living she sought him not, nor dreamed that fate
For any subterfuge would swing my gate.
Loving, she gave herself to livid death,
Joyous she bought his respite with her breath,
Came, not embodied, but a tenuous shade,
In whom her rapture a great radiance made.
For never saw I ghost upon this shore
Shine with such living ecstasy before,
Nor heard an exile from the light above
Hail me with smiles: ***Thou art not Death but Love!***

"But when the gods, frustrated, this beheld,
How, living still, among the dead she dwelled,
Because she lived in him whose life she won,
And her blood beat in his beneath the sun,
They reasoned: 'When the bitter Stygian wave
The sweetness of love's kisses cannot lave,
When the pale flood of Lethe washes not
From mortal mind one high immortal thought,
Akin to us the earthly creature grows,
Since nature suffers only what it knows.
If she whom we to this grey desert banned
Still dreams she treads with him the sunlit land
That for his sake she left without a tear,
Set wide the gates--her being is not here.'

"So ruled the gods; but thou, that sought'st to give
Thy life for love, yet for thyself wouldst live.
They know not for their kin; but back to earth
Give, pitying, one that is of mortal birth."

Humbled the Harper heard, and turned away,
Mounting alone to the empoverished day;
Yet, as he left the Stygian shades behind,
He heard the cordage on the harbour wind,
Saw the blue smoke above the homestead trees,
And in his hidden heart was glad of these.

AN AUTUMN SUNSET

I

LEAGUERED in fire
The wild black promontories of the coast extend
Their savage silhouettes;
The sun in universal carnage sets,
And, halting higher,
The motionless storm-clouds mass their sullen threats,
Like an advancing mob in sword-points penned,
That, balked, yet stands at bay.
Mid-zenith hangs the fascinated day
In wind-lustrated hollows crystalline,
A wan Valkyrie whose wide pinions shine
Across the ensanguined ruins of the fray,
And in her hand swings high o'erhead,
Above the waste of war,
The silver torch-light of the evening star
Wherewith to search the faces of the dead.

II

Lagooned in gold,
Seem not those jetty promontories rather
The outposts of some ancient land forlorn,
Uncomforted of morn,
Where old oblivions gather,
The melancholy unconsoling fold
Of all things that go utterly to death
And mix no more, no more
With life's perpetually awakening breath?
Shall Time not ferry me to such a shore,
Over such sailless seas,
To walk with hope's slain importunities
In miserable marriage? Nay, shall not
All things be there forgot,
Save the sea's golden barrier and the black
Close-crouching promontories?
Dead to all shames, forgotten of all glories,
Shall I not wander there, a shadow's shade,
A spectre self-destroyed,
So purged of all remembrance and sucked back
Into the primal void,
That should we on that shore phantasmal meet
I should not know the coming of your feet?

MOONRISE OVER TYRINGHAM

NOW the high holocaust of hours is done,
And all the west empurpled with their death,
How swift oblivion drinks the fallen sun,
How little while the dusk remembereth!

Though some there were, proud hours that marched in mail,
And took the morning on auspicious crest,
Crying to fortune "Back, for I prevail!"--
Yet now they lie disfeatured with the rest;

And some that stole so soft on destiny
Methought they had surprised her to a smile;
But these fled frozen when she turned to see,
And moaned and muttered through my heart awhile.

But now the day is emptied of them all,
And night absorbs their life-blood at a draught;
And so my life lies, as the gods let fall
An empty cup from which their lips have quaffed.

Yet see--night is not . . . by translucent ways,
Up the grey void of autumn afternoon
Steals a mild crescent, charioted in haze,
And all the air is merciful as June.

The lake is a forgotten streak of day
That trembles through the hemlocks' darkling bars,
And still, my heart, still some divine delay
Upon the threshold holds the earliest stars.

O pale equivocal hour, whose suppliant feet
Haunt the mute reaches of the sleeping wind,
Art thou a watcher stealing to entreat
Prayer and sepulture for thy fallen kind?

Poor plaintive waif of a predestined race,
Their ruin gapes for thee. Why linger here?
Go hence in silence. Veil thine orphaned face,
Lest I should look on it and call it dear.

For if I love thee thou wilt sooner die;
Some sudden ruin will plunge upon thy head,
Midnight will fall from the revengeful sky
And hurl thee down among thy shuddering dead.

Avert thine eyes. Lapse softly from my sight,
Call not my name, nor heed if thine I crave,
So shalt thou sink through mitigated night
And bathe thee in the all-effacing wave.

But upward still thy perilous footsteps fare
Along a high-hung heaven drenched in light,
Dilating on a tide of crystal air
That floods the dark hills to their utmost height.

Strange hour, is this thy waning face that leans
Out of mid-heaven and makes my soul its glass?
What victory is imaged there? What means
Thy tarrying smile? Oh, veil thy lips and pass.

Nay . . . pause and let me name thee! For I see,
O with what flooding ecstasy of light,
Strange hour that wilt not loose thy hold on me,

Thou'rt not day's latest, but the first of night!

And after thee the gold-foot stars come thick,
From hand to hand they toss the flying fire,
Till all the zenith with their dance is quick
About the wheeling music of the Lyre.

Dread hour that lead'st the immemorial round,
With lifted torch revealing one by one
The thronging splendours that the day held bound,
And how each blue abyss enshrines its sun--

Be thou the image of a thought that fares
Forth from itself, and flings its ray ahead,
Leaping the barriers of ephemeral cares,
To where our lives are but the ages' tread,

And let this year be, not the last of youth,
But first--like thee!--of some new train of hours,
If more remote from hope, yet nearer truth,
And kin to the unpetitionable powers.

ALL SOULS

I

A THIN moon faints in the sky o'erhead,
And dumb in the churchyard lie the dead.
Walk we not, Sweet, by garden ways,
Where the late rose hangs and the phlox delays,
But forth of the gate and down the road,
Past the church and the yews, to their dim abode.
For it's turn of the year and All Souls' night,
When the dead can hear and the dead have sight.

II

Fear not that sound like wind in the trees:
It is only their call that comes on the breeze;
Fear not the shudder that seems to pass:
It is only the tread of their feet on the grass;
Fear not the drip of the bough as you stoop:
It is only the touch of their hands that grope
For the year's on the turn and it's All Souls' night,
When the dead can yearn and the dead can smite.

III

And where should a man bring his sweet to woo
But here, where such hundreds were lovers too?
Where lie the dead lips that thirst to kiss,

The empty hands that their fellows miss,
Where the maid and her lover, from sere to green,
Sleep bed by bed, with the worm between?
For it's turn of the year and All Souls' night,
When the dead can hear and the dead have sight.

IV

And now they rise and walk in the cold,
Let us warm their blood and give youth to the old.
Let them see us and hear us, and say: "Ah, thus
In the prime of the year it went with us!"
Till their lips drawn close, and so long unkist,
Forget they are mist that mingles with mist!
For the year's on the turn, and it's All Souls' night,
When the dead can burn and the dead can smite.

V

Till they say, as they hear us--poor dead, poor dead!--
"Just an hour of this, and our age-long bed--
Just a thrill of the old remembered pains
To kindle a flame in our frozen veins,
A touch, and a sight, and a floating apart,
As the chill of dawn strikes each phantom heart--
For it's turn of the year and All Souls' night,
When the dead can hear and the dead have sight."

VI

And where should the living feel alive
But here in this wan white humming hive,
As the moon wastes down, and the dawn turns cold,
And one by one they creep back to the fold?
And where should a man hold his mate and say:
"One more, one more, ere we go their way"?
For the year's on the turn, and it's All Souls' night,
When the living can learn by the churchyard light.

VII

And how should we break faith who have seen
Those dead lips plight with the mist between,
And how forget, who have seen how soon
They lie thus chambered and cold to the moon?
How scorn, how hate, how strive, wee too,
Who must do so soon as those others do?
For it's All Souls' night, and break of the day,
And behold, with the light the dead are away. . .

ALL SAINTS

ALL so grave and shining see they come
From the blissful ranks of the forgiven,
Though so distant wheels the nearest crystal dome,
And the spheres are seven.

Are you in such haste to come to earth,
Shining ones, the Wonder on your brow,
To the low poor places of your birth,
And the day that must be darkness now?

Does the heart still crave the spot it yearned on
In the grey and mortal years,
The pure flame the smoky hearth it burned on,
The clear eye its tears?

Was there, in the narrow range of living,
After all the wider scope?
In the old old rapture of forgiving,
In the long long flight of hope?

Come you, from free sweep across the spaces,
To the irksome bounds of mortal law,
From the all-embracing Vision, to some face's
Look that never saw?

Never we, imprisoned here, had sought you,
Lured you with the ancient bait of pain,
Down the silver current of the light-years brought you

To the beaten round again--

Is it you, perchance, who ache to strain us
Dumbly to the dim transfigured breast,
Or with tragic gesture would detain us
From the age-long search for rest?

Is the labour then more glorious than the laurel,
The learning than the conquered thought?
Is the meed of men the righteous quarrel,
Not the justice wrought?

Long ago we guessed it, faithful ghosts,
Proudly chose the present for our scene,
And sent out indomitable hosts
Day by day to widen our demesne.

Sit you by our hearth-stone, lone immortals,
Share again the bitter wine of life!
Well we know, beyond the peaceful portals
There is nothing better than our strife,

Nought more thrilling than the cry that calls us,
Spent and stumbling, to the conflict vain,
After each disaster that befalls us
Nerves us for a sterner strain.

And, when flood or foeman shakes the sleeper
In his moment's lapse from pain,
Bids us fold our tents, and flee our kin, and deeper
Drive into the wilderness again.

THE OLD POLE STAR

BEFORE the clepsydra had bound the days
Man tethered Change to his fixed star, and said:
"The elder races, that long since are dead,
Marched by that light; it swerves not from its base
Though all the worlds about it wax and fade."

When Egypt saw it, fast in reeling spheres,
Her Pyramids shaft-centred on its ray
She reared and said: "Long as this star holds sway
In uninvaded ether, shall the years
Revere my monuments--" and went her way.

The Pyramids abide; but through the shaft
That held the polar pivot, eye to eye,
Look now--blank nothingness! As though Change laughed
At man's presumption and his puny craft,
The star has slipped its leash and roams the sky.

Yet could the immemorial piles be swung
A skyey hair's-breadth from their rooted base,
Back to the central anchorage of space,
Ah, then again, as when the race was young,
Should they behold the beacon of the race!

Of old, men said: "The Truth is there: we rear
Our faith full-centred on it. It was known
Thus of the elders who foreran us here,
Mapped out its circuit in the shifting sphere,
And found it, 'mid mutation, fixed alone."

Change laughs again, again the sky is cold,
And down that fissure now no star-beam glides.
Yet they whose sweep of vision grows not old
Still at the central point of space behold
Another pole-star: for the Truth abides.

A GRAVE

THOUGH life should come
With all its marshalled honours, trump and drum,
To proffer you the captaincy of some
Resounding exploit, that shall fill
Man's pulses with commemorative thrill,
And be a banner to far battle days
For truths unrisen upon untrod ways,
What would your answer be,
O heart once brave?
Seek otherwhere; for me,
I watch beside a grave.

Though to some shining festival of thought
The sages call you from steep citadel
Of bastioned argument, whose rampart gained
Yields the pure vision passionately sought,
In dreams known well,
But never yet in wakefulness attained,
How should you answer to their summons, save:
I watch beside a grave?

Though Beauty, from her fane within the soul
Of fire-tongued seers descending,
Or from the dream-lit temples of the past
With feet immortal wending,
Illuminate grief's antre swart and vast
With half-veiled face that promises the whole
To him who holds her fast,
What answer could you give?
Sight of one face I crave,
One only while I live;
Woo elsewhere; for I watch beside a grave.

Though love of the one heart that loves you best,
A storm-tossed messenger,
Should beat its wings for shelter in your breast,
Where clung its last year's nest,
The nest you built together and made fast
Lest envious winds should stir,
And winged each delicate thought to minister
With sweetness far-amassed
To the young dreams within--
What answer could it win?
The nest was whelmed in sorrow's rising wave,
Nor could I reach one drowning dream to save;
I watch beside a grave.

NON DOLET!

AGE after age the fruit of knowledge falls
To ashes on men's lips;
Love fails, faith sickens, like a dying tree
Life sheds its dreams that no new spring recalls;
The longed-for ships
Come empty home or founder on the deep,
And eyes first lose their tears and then their sleep.

So weary a world it lies, forlorn of day,
And yet not wholly dark,
Since evermore some soul that missed the mark
Calls back to those agrope
In the mad maze of hope,
"Courage, my brothers--I have found the way!"

The day is lost? What then?
What though the straggling rear-guard of the fight
Be whelmed in fear and night,
And the flying scouts proclaim
That death has gripped the van--
Ever the heart of man
Cheers on the hearts of men!

"It hurts not!" dying cried the Roman wife;
And one by one
The leaders in the strife
Fall on the blade of failure and exclaim:
"The day is won!"

A HUNTING-SONG

HUNTERS, *where does Hope nest?*
Not in the half-oped breast,
Nor the young rose,
Nor April sunrise--those
With a quick wing she brushes,
The wide world through,
Greets with the throat of thrushes,
Fades from as fast as dew.

But, would you spy her sleeping,
Cradled warm,
Look in the breast of weeping,
The tree stript by storm;
But, would you bind her fast,
Yours at last,
Bed-mate and lover,
Gain the last headland bare
That the cold tides cover,
There may you capture her, there,
Where the sea gives to the ground
Only the drift of the drowned.
Yet, if she slips you, once found,
Push to her uttermost lair
In the low house of despair.
There will she watch by your head,
Sing to you till you be dead,
Then, with your child in her breast,
In another heart build a new nest.

SURVIVAL

WHEN you and I, like all things kind or cruel,
The garnered days and light evasive hours,
Are gone again to be a part of flowers
And tears and tides, in life's divine renewal,

If some grey eve to certain eyes should wear
A deeper radiance than mere light can give,
Some silent page abruptly flush and live,
May it not be that you and I are there?

USES

AH, from the niggard tree of Time
How quickly fall the hours!
It needs no touch of wind or rime
To loose such facile flowers.

Drift of the dead year's harvesting,
They clog to-morrow's way,
Yet serve to shelter growths of spring
Beneath their warm decay,

Or, blent by pious hands with rare
Sweet savours of content,

Surprise the soul's December air
With June's forgotten scent.

A MEETING

ON a sheer peak of joy we meet;
Below us hums the abyss;
Death either way allures our feet
If we take one step amiss.

One moment let us drink the blue
Transcendent air together--
Then down where the same old work's to do
In the same dull daily weather.

We may not wait . . . yet look below!
How part? On this keen ridge
But one may pass. They call you--go!
My life shall be your bridge.

Note.--Vesalius, the great anatomist, studied at Louvain and Paris, and was called by Venice to the chair of surgery in the University of Padua. He was one of the first physiologists to dissect the human body, and his great work "The Structure of the Human Body" was an open attack on the physiology of Galen. The book excited such violent opposition, not only in the Church but in the University, that in a fit of discouragement he burned his remaining manuscripts and accepted the post of physician at the Court of Charles V., and afterward of his son, Philip II, of Spain. This closed his life of free enquiry, for the Inquisition forbade all scientific research, and the dissection of corpses was prohibited in Spain. Vesalius led for many years the life of the rich and successful court physician, but regrets for his past were never wholly extinguished, and in 1561 they were roused afresh by the reading of an anatomical treatise by Gabriel Fallopius, his successor in the chair at Padua. From that moment life in Spain became intolerable to Vesalius, and in 1563 he set out for the East. Tradition reports that this journey was a penance to which the Church condemned him for having opened the body of a woman before she was actually dead; but more probably Vesalius, sick of his long servitude, made the pilgrimage a pretext to escape from Spain.

Fallopius had meanwhile died, and the Venetian Senate is said to have offered Vesalius his old chair; but on the way home from Jerusalem he was seized with illness, and died at Zante in 1564.

The Codes Of Hammurabi And Moses
W. W. Davies

QTY

The discovery of the Hammurabi Code is one of the greatest achievements of archaeology, and is of paramount interest, not only to the student of the Bible, but also to all those interested in ancient history...

Religion   **ISBN:** *1-59462-338-4*   **Pages:132**
MSRP $12.95

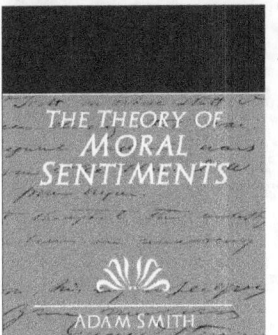

The Theory of Moral Sentiments
Adam Smith

QTY

This work from 1749. contains original theories of conscience amd moral judgment and it is the foundation for systemof morals.

Philosophy   **ISBN:** *1-59462-777-0*   **Pages:536**
MSRP $19.95

Jessica's First Prayer
Hesba Stretton

QTY

In a screened and secluded corner of one of the many railway-bridges which span the streets of London there could be seen a few years ago, from five o'clock every morning until half past eight, a tidily set-out coffee-stall, consisting of a trestle and board, upon which stood two large tin cans, with a small fire of charcoal burning under each so as to keep the coffee boiling during the early hours of the morning when the work-people were thronging into the city on their way to their daily toil...

Pages:84

Childrens   **ISBN:** *1-59462-373-2*   *MSRP $9.95*

My Life and Work
Henry Ford

QTY

Henry Ford revolutionized the world with his implementation of mass production for the Model T automobile. Gain valuable business insight into his life and work with his own auto-biography... "We have only started on our development of our country we have not as yet, with all our talk of wonderful progress, done more than scratch the surface. The progress has been wonderful enough but..."

Pages:300

Biographies/   **ISBN:** *1-59462-198-5*   *MSRP $21.95*

The Art of Cross-Examination
Francis Wellman

QTY

I presume it is the experience of every author, after his first book is published upon an important subject, to be almost overwhelmed with a wealth of ideas and illustrations which could readily have been included in his book, and which to his own mind, at least, seem to make a second edition inevitable. Such certainly was the case with me; and when the first edition had reached its sixth impression in five months, I rejoiced to learn that it seemed to my publishers that the book had met with a sufficiently favorable reception to justify a second and considerably enlarged edition. ...

Pages:412

Reference   ISBN: *1-59462-647-2*   *MSRP $19.95*

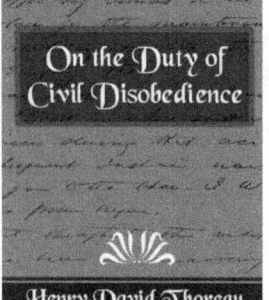

On the Duty of Civil Disobedience
Henry David Thoreau

QTY

Thoreau wrote his famous essay, On the Duty of Civil Disobedience, as a protest against an unjust but popular war and the immoral but popular institution of slave-owning. He did more than write—he declined to pay his taxes, and was hauled off to gaol in consequence. Who can say how much this refusal of his hastened the end of the war and of slavery ?

Law   ISBN: *1-59462-747-9*   **Pages:48**   *MSRP $7.45*

Dream Psychology
Psychoanalysis for Beginners

Sigmund Freud

Dream Psychology Psychoanalysis for Beginners
Sigmund Freud

QTY

Sigmund Freud, born Sigismund Schlomo Freud (May 6, 1856 - September 23, 1939), was a Jewish-Austrian neurologist and psychiatrist who co-founded the psychoanalytic school of psychology. Freud is best known for his theories of the unconscious mind, especially involving the mechanism of repression; his redefinition of sexual desire as mobile and directed towards a wide variety of objects; and his therapeutic techniques, especially his understanding of transference in the therapeutic relationship and the presumed value of dreams as sources of insight into unconscious desires.

Pages:196

Psychology   ISBN: *1-59462-905-6*   *MSRP $15.45*

The Miracle of Right Thought
Orison Swett Marden

QTY

Believe with all of your heart that you will do what you were made to do. When the mind has once formed the habit of holding cheerful, happy, prosperous pictures, it will not be easy to form the opposite habit. It does not matter how improbable or how far away this realization may see, or how dark the prospects may be, if we visualize them as best we can, as vividly as possible, hold tenaciously to them and vigorously struggle to attain them, they will gradually become actualized, realized in the life. But a desire, a longing without endeavor, a yearning abandoned or held indifferently will vanish without realization.

Pages:360

Self Help   ISBN: *1-59462-644-8*   *MSRP $25.45*

QTY

The Rosicrucian Cosmo-Conception Mystic Christianity *by Max Heindel*   ISBN: *1-59462-188-8*   **$38.95**
The Rosicrucian Cosmo-conception is not dogmatic, neither does it appeal to any other authority than the reason of the student. It is: not controversial, but is: sent forth in the, hope that it may help to clear...   New Age/Religion Pages 646

Abandonment To Divine Providence *by Jean-Pierre de Caussade*   ISBN: *1-59462-228-0*   **$25.95**
"The Rev. Jean Pierre de Caussade was one of the most remarkable spiritual writers of the Society of Jesus in France in the 18th Century. His death took place at Toulouse in 1751. His works have gone through many editions and have been republished...   Inspirational/Religion Pages 400

Mental Chemistry *by Charles Haanel*   ISBN: *1-59462-192-6*   **$23.95**
Mental Chemistry allows the change of material conditions by combining and appropriately utilizing the power of the mind. Much like applied chemistry creates something new and unique out of careful combinations of chemicals the mastery of mental chemistry...   New Age Pages 354

The Letters of Robert Browning and Elizabeth Barret Barrett 1845-1846 vol II   ISBN: *1-59462-193-4*   **$35.95**
by Robert Browning and Elizabeth Barrett   Biographies Pages 596

Gleanings In Genesis (volume I) *by Arthur W. Pink*   ISBN: *1-59462-130-6*   **$27.45**
Appropriately has Genesis been termed "the seed plot of the Bible" for in it we have, in germ form, almost all of the great doctrines which are afterwards fully developed in the books of Scripture which follow...   Religion/Inspirational Pages 420

The Master Key *by L. W. de Laurence*   ISBN: *1-59462-001-6*   **$30.95**
In no branch of human knowledge has there been a more lively increase of the spirit of research during the past few years than in the study of Psychology, Concentration and Mental Discipline. The requests for authentic lessons in Thought Control, Mental Discipline and...   New Age/Business Pages 422

The Lesser Key Of Solomon Goetia *by L. W. de Laurence*   ISBN: *1-59462-092-X*   **$9.95**
This translation of the first book of the "Lernegton" which is now for the first time made accessible to students of Talismanic Magic was done, after careful collation and edition, from numerous Ancient Manuscripts in Hebrew, Latin, and French...   New Age/Occult Pages 92

Rubaiyat Of Omar Khayyam *by Edward Fitzgerald*   ISBN:*1-59462-332-5*   **$13.95**
Edward Fitzgerald, whom the world has already learned, in spite of his own efforts to remain within the shadow of anonymity, to look upon as one of the rarest poets of the century, was born at Bredfield, in Suffolk, on the 31st of March, 1809. He was the third son of John Purcell...   Music Pages 172

Ancient Law *by Henry Maine*   ISBN: *1-59462-128-4*   **$29.95**
The chief object of the following pages is to indicate some of the earliest ideas of mankind, as they are reflected in Ancient Law, and to point out the relation of those ideas to modern thought.   Religion/History Pages 452

Far-Away Stories *by William J. Locke*   ISBN: *1-59462-129-2*   **$19.45**
"Good wine needs no bush, but a collection of mixed vintages does. And this book is just such a collection. Some of the stories I do not want to remain buried for ever in the museum files of dead magazine-numbers an author's not unpardonable vanity..."   Fiction Pages 272

Life of David Crockett *by David Crockett*   ISBN: *1-59462-250-7*   **$27.45**
"Colonel David Crockett was one of the most remarkable men of the times in which he lived. Born in humble life, but gifted with a strong will, an indomitable courage, and unremitting perseverance...   Biographies/New Age Pages 424

Lip-Reading *by Edward Nitchie*   ISBN: *1-59462-206-X*   **$25.95**
Edward B. Nitchie, founder of the New York School for the Hard of Hearing, now the Nitchie School of Lip-Reading, Inc, wrote "LIP-READING Principles and Practice". The development and perfecting of this meritorious work on lip-reading was an undertaking...   How-to Pages 400

A Handbook of Suggestive Therapeutics, Applied Hypnotism, Psychic Science   ISBN: *1-59462-214-0*   **$24.95**
by Henry Munro   Health/New Age/Health/Self-help Pages 376

A Doll's House: and Two Other Plays *by Henrik Ibsen*   ISBN: *1-59462-112-8*   **$19.95**
Henrik Ibsen created this classic when in revolutionary 1848 Rome. Introducing some striking concepts in playwriting for the realist genre, this play has been studied the world over.   Fiction/Classics/Plays 308

The Light of Asia *by sir Edwin Arnold*   ISBN: *1-59462-204-3*   **$13.95**
In this poetic masterpiece, Edwin Arnold describes the life and teachings of Buddha. The man who was to become known as Buddha to the world was born as Prince Gautama of India but he rejected the worldly riches and abandoned the reigns of power when...   Religion/History/Biographies Pages 170

The Complete Works of Guy de Maupassant *by Guy de Maupassant*   ISBN: *1-59462-157-8*   **$16.95**
"For days and days, nights and nights, I had dreamed of that first kiss which was to consecrate our engagement, and I knew not on what spot I should put my lips..."   Fiction/Classics Pages 240

The Art of Cross-Examination *by Francis L. Wellman*   ISBN: *1-59462-309-0*   **$26.95**
Written by a renowned trial lawyer, Wellman imparts his experience and uses case studies to explain how to use psychology to extract desired information through questioning.   How-to/Science/Reference Pages 408

Answered or Unanswered? *by Louisa Vaughan*   ISBN: *1-59462-248-5*   **$10.95**
Miracles of Faith in China   Religion Pages 112

The Edinburgh Lectures on Mental Science (1909) *by Thomas*   ISBN: *1-59462-008-3*   **$11.95**
This book contains the substance of a course of lectures recently given by the writer in the Queen Street Hail, Edinburgh. Its purpose is to indicate the Natural Principles governing the relation between Mental Action and Material Conditions...   New Age/Psychology Pages 148

Ayesha *by H. Rider Haggard*   ISBN: *1-59462-301-5*   **$24.95**
Verily and indeed it is the unexpected that happens! Probably if there was one person upon the earth from whom the Editor of this, and of a certain previous history, did not expect to hear again...   Classics Pages 380

Ayala's Angel *by Anthony Trollope*   ISBN: *1-59462-352-X*   **$29.95**
The two girls were both pretty, but Lucy who was twenty-one who supposed to be simple and comparatively unattractive, whereas Ayala was credited, as her Bombwhat romantic name might show, with poetic charm and a taste for romance. Ayala when her father died was nineteen...   Fiction Pages 484

The American Commonwealth *by James Bryce*   ISBN: *1-59462-286-8*   **$34.45**
An interpretation of American democratic political theory. It examines political mechanics and society from the perspective of Scotsman James Bryce   Politics Pages 572

Stories of the Pilgrims *by Margaret P. Pumphrey*   ISBN: *1-59462-116-0*   **$17.95**
This book explores pilgrims religious oppression in England as well as their escape to Holland and eventual crossing to America on the Mayflower, and their early days in New England...   History Pages 268

QTY

The Fasting Cure *by Sinclair Upton* — ISBN: *1-59462-222-1* **$13.95**
In the Cosmopolitan Magazine for May, 1910, and in the Contemporary Review (London) for April, 1910, I published an article dealing with my experiences in fasting. I have written a great many magazine articles, but never one which attracted so much attention... New Age/Self Help/Health Pages 164

Hebrew Astrology *by Sepharial* — ISBN: *1-59462-308-2* **$13.45**
In these days of advanced thinking it is a matter of common observation that we have left many of the old landmarks behind and that we are now pressing forward to greater heights and to a wider horizon than that which represented the mind-content of our progenitors... Astrology Pages 144

Thought Vibration or The Law of Attraction in the Thought World — ISBN: *1-59462-127-6* **$12.95**
by William Walker Atkinson — Psychology/Religion Pages 144

Optimism *by Helen Keller* — ISBN: *1-59462-108-X* **$15.95**
Helen Keller was blind, deaf, and mute since 19 months old, yet famously learned how to overcome these handicaps, communicate with the world, and spread her lectures promoting optimism. An inspiring read for everyone... Biographies/Inspirational Pages 84

Sara Crewe *by Frances Burnett* — ISBN: *1-59462-360-0* **$9.45**
In the first place, Miss Minchin lived in London. Her home was a large, dull, tall one, in a large, dull square, where all the houses were alike, and all the sparrows were alike, and where all the door-knockers made the same heavy sound... Childrens/Classic Pages 88

The Autobiography of Benjamin Franklin *by Benjamin Franklin* — ISBN: *1-59462-135-7* **$24.95**
The Autobiography of Benjamin Franklin has probably been more extensively read than any other American historical work, and no other book of its kind has had such ups and downs of fortune. Franklin lived for many years in England, where he was agent... Biographies/History Pages 332

Name	
Email	
Telephone	
Address	
City, State ZIP	

☐ Credit Card   ☐ Check / Money Order

Credit Card Number	
Expiration Date	
Signature	

Please Mail to: Book Jungle
PO Box 2226
Champaign, IL 61825
or Fax to: 630-214-0564

ORDERING INFORMATION
web*: www.bookjungle.com*
email*: sales@bookjungle.com*
fax*: 630-214-0564*
mail*: Book Jungle PO Box 2226 Champaign, IL 61825*
or PayPal *to sales@bookjungle.com*

Please contact us for bulk discounts

DIRECT-ORDER TERMS
20% Discount if You Order Two or More Books
Free Domestic Shipping!
Accepted: Master Card, Visa, Discover, American Express

www.ingramcontent.com/pod-product-compliance
Lightning Source LLC
Chambersburg PA
CBHW081305200626
46813CB00018B/3259